HECATE'S FAUN

by

Marc Royston

ISBN: 0692507701

ISBN-13: 978-0692507704 (My Boy Publishing)

<u>DEDICATION</u>

For All Who Stand Beside Me Through Adversity.

My Family.

My Friends.

I Thank You.

HECATE'S FAUN

They think me a willow, languorous, bending in grief for the

lost sons of the confederacy, like so many wives and mothers

left behind, suffocating beneath the stifling swelter of yet

another Georgian summer, and pining for a return to a glory

the South is loath to accept as vanquished.

Anemic, I pale whiter than Irish lace—and almost as

bloodless as the corpse floating in my pond, his face a faded

effigy cast in eternal slumber.

Were he a soldier wandered home to die, I'd rest him to

his grave and grant him rite of scripture, no matter the flag

under which he marched. Whatever their allegiance on earth,

all souls belong to God, so how am I to judge any less? From

the ever-shifting ranks, we've seen so many straggle across

our lands, both the shattered blue and the broken grey. We've

cringed at the crackling muskets and gagged on the smoke of

torch and cannon. The cries of the infantry howling for retreat and of the officers bellowing for rally yet ring from the distant woods, echoing in our dreams. We've recoiled from each bloody breeze, the taste of death a burning stone which choked our every breath. We've clapped our ears against the bugle's bray and to muffle the beat of the marching drums, and we've heard the dying scream.

But this body, howsoever human it resembled, drifting belly-up in my pond and snagged naked against the reeds, soaked to a shine and blissfully at peace, was nothing ever of woman born.

Upon my widening eyes, his reflection and all its impossibilities sharply focused.

Within the wells of his unblinking regard, sideways slits of obsidian across twin beds of fractured amber, I saw myself likewise mirrored, as though I glimpsed the view perceived by his lingering spirit.

When I stare, people startle, for they are astonished by my gaze, irises as grey as powdered cinder. They find my silence threatening and my mourning a shadow too ominous to be entered. My touch is avoided for fear of contracting the smallest share of my damnation. And so, I am long accustomed as a hermit, keeping to my home, and treated only by flutters of brainless gossip and to the occasional gawking of my neighbors. My needs are few; my infrequent goods delivered; and I gave up church long ago. I have little recourse to companionship or to chatter and almost no contact beyond my gate. However, as is widely known from the borders of my lands and all the way to the county seat, wherever my name is spoken, I have resigned humanity, and humanity has abandoned me.

At the world's edge, I am an outpost, keeping watch upon oblivion, solitary in my vigil.

They whisper that I smell of hyacinth and that I once danced with an eastern Prince. They say you wouldn't know it, but I was a fabled beauty with suitors lined upon my porch. My snowy mane once flowed as long as any debutante's and glistened as black as pitch. My wrinkled skin once was smooth and my dappled complexion unblemished. I wore resplendent jewels and softest silk, and my gowns were sewn across the Atlantic, and the like were worn only by the wealthiest heirs to nobility. When I laughed, the world spun brighter, and my name was all the invitation needed to open any door. They say my family founded an empire upon sugar cane and rum and that we lived fast and hard, our heritage corrupted by the taint of gypsy blood and by the juju of the darkest slaves. But they also say we knew our verses. We said our prayers and paid our tithes equal to the most devout. Our table was set for any stranger, and we always stoked charity in our hearts. Yet they whisper behind closed doors that my last relations long since disappeared or have died of an unspoken shame. In a single night, whether freemen or slaves, man, woman, or child, all deserted my plantation, never to be seen or heard again, and, now, I am my only tenant. They say only crows will nest in the leafless branches of my many groves, and neither hound nor hare shall trespass upon my domain. Even the wind abhors a visit, and the only songs heard above my estate are the shrill caws of a black flock of feathered devils that laugh in mockery of my fallow fields.

But it is for my failures that I languish, not for banishment by Man or Nature, not for war or lover lost, not for any history of my bloodline, whether real or imagined, nor for any so-called fall from God or grace. I simply bow in surrender to my fate and in recognition of my deficiency to prosper in this unfriendly world.

I have lost the strength to struggle or even to protest.

A creature of moonlight, a denizen of dimensions in-between, an explorer of deepest reverie, I stalk through the brambles of my plantation. Only when the stars hang high do I step out-of-doors, for only then am I free. No passing eyes to follow from the distant roads. No fingers to point. My thoughts in mist gently fall. And my melancholy scents the air with sorrows too bitter to be inhaled.

Do not think me a phantom as I glide, a silhouette slipping mutely through the night. Many times, I have been so mistaken. But I haunt only myself. Do not think me an unhappy dream. I live inside delusion, but I am its maker and not its result. Straddling both past and present, I exist in two worlds at once. Absent fulfillment in either, I am hopeless of meaningful conclusion.

I am just another cursed soul wending from day-to-day, one of a countless and uncounted population, too much a coward to shape my fate or to accept my circumstance or to end my futile existence.

I am of listless wit and bled of vigor.

It is in this perpetual state of self-absorption and morbid contemplation that I discovered *him*.

Within a thicket at the heart of my dominion, the pond had been a haven for generations, for the meditations of my forebears and for their recreation. In my younger days, my sisters and I splashed in its brackish waters. Fish had once been plentiful and bent many a lazy pole. A rowboat, long since rotted, now abandoned in the muck, had once been roped to a small pier. Those planks had collapsed years ago, and only the stunted pylons remained. Picnics had oft been held for idle pleasures upon the muddy shore. And from the surrounding canopy, birdsong had merrily twittered.

But now the place smelled of ruin and decay; and the pool lay flat and silver, isolated and silent. Starlight reflected from the surface, like fireflies stitched into a silken sheet of black that had been stained in smears of sickly green. Off this dull mirror, a sliver of moon brightly shimmered, a crescent brushed in a poisonous blur of white.

You could hardly see the horns jutting from the cadaver's brow. But there they were. They didn't even surprise me all that much. I can't say why they didn't. But I looked long to make certain. Blunt and small, indistinguishable from the buds of a young goat, each tip sprouted into a subtle curve.

He seemed both real and unreal, like one of Tussaud's waxen dolls in that frightening museum of hers where villains and heroes alike stand captured in perpetuity. He should have lurched into life when glimpsed. He should have risen. I held my breath in expectation, but his chest neither rose nor fell.

Pallid, his chiseled face reposed in serenity. Like a pair of graceful swans, his hands gently drifted. He had the fingers of an artist, long and elegant, and nails well-clipped and clean. From a distance, he still might have been taken for human, were it not for his bobbing hooves and the backwards bend at his knees. He belonged to a race as much beast as it was cousin to mankind.

I should have been dismayed. But I was not. In him, I saw something familiar, perhaps a kindred spirit. Or maybe I was just taken by the tragedy, too overcome with concern for a life untimely claimed.

With a plunge, I waded into the lukewarm waters and grabbed him beneath his arms. Awkwardly, fighting the volume of my gown, I staggered backwards and dragged his dead weight up the embankment. As I knelt at his side, I checked frantically for a pulse. On neck and wrist, I pressed. Upon his chest, I laid my head and listened.

But had he a heart, it no longer beat. Nor could I discern an injury. I feared this poor creature had wandered into the middle of a confrontation and had been caught in the crossfire. Or I feared he had been assaulted by some superstitious fool who came upon him in the heat of battle or in a moment of unthinking terror. I feared that amidst the relentless conflict he had been unable to forage and so at last had starved only a few hundred yards from my larder. But other than his lack of motion, he looked hale and whole. And young. Were he fully human, I would have said he had not yet grown a man.

His skin was only barely chilled. He could not have expired that long ago.

Scrambling, I rolled him to his hip. I considered the possibility that he might have run recklessly in fear of the thundering cannons, loud even when miles away, and stumbled in the dark, falling into this pool before he ever saw it. If he didn't know how to swim or if his strange physique deprived him of the ability, he would have drowned. Under this theory, I concluded I must evacuate his lungs with all haste. Had I happened upon him soon enough, I still might summon his return. If only he could be coerced to respire yet again, I might see his foreign intelligence alive and looking back at me. We might even converse. Or did he ever possess the capacity for speech? For so fabulous a creation, my questions mounted without end. I choked on their congestion.

But no matter how hard I thumped his back or dug my finger down his throat, he neither coughed nor sputtered, and not a single drop escaped his rounded lips.

I rolled him once more to his spine, and hammered my fist upon his chest. I pinched his nostrils, and, with my mouth sealed to his, I exhaled. Again and again, I fought to raise my Lazarus.

In the distance, a scattering of bullets fired. Their patter profaned the night. But the perfect quiet returned like a displaced tar. For minutes, only my breath and the beating of my fist made any sound.

The steaming atmosphere clung to my skin, and the heavy skies pressed upon me.

What was he? Did he have a name? Where did he come from? Why did he leave? Were there more of his kind or was he a singularity? Did anyone worry about his fate? Did he suffer? How is it he came to me? How did he meet his end? What was his last thought? Or his last wish?

With each ballooning of his matted chest, I silently inquired, desperate to uncover his many secrets.

And the night began to whisper.

As though spewed from the confusion of a laudanum dream, the scenery twisted. Clouds gathered, deepening the dim. In spasms of anguish, the landscape writhed, an amorphous pastiche that swirled in tones of liquid grey and limbo black. Trees bowed as though forever falling yet never toppled to the ground. To every side, silhouettes shuddered. Like a nest of serpents expanding without limit, the distortion enshrouded the thicket and covered the pond.

The laughter of a young girl briefly burst.

"Gigi?" I asked the night.

But my premonition came nearly too late. And, as always, I was its only witness. I bolted to my feet and stepped forward, hoping that my skirt, although damp and sagging between the hoops, would be enough to mask the body at my back. I could do nothing to camouflage my dousing other than rely on blending with the shadowed night.

The intruder broke his cover. "Evening," a voice weathered by decades rasped, grinding any vestige of tranquility into splinters. Immediately, the landscape settled. And the girl's laughter faded.

Out of the surrounding void, a hulking figure on horseback emerged. It loped from the nearest edge of the spindled woods and headed toward me. The steed was black, and the man was grey. In his saddle, an old soldier slumped, bouncing to his horse's weary gait. As he came to within several yards, my caller tipped his cap in greeting. Upon his breast, a flowering stain faintly glistened. Spattered and poorly lit, the wet blood looked like a ragged hole in his chest.

Exerting effort, the old soldier raised his head and fixed me with a rheumy squint.

On the distant horizon, the sky blushed brighter, welling with the glow of a burning city. There, the heavens thickened, and a rising blur hid the stars behind its fog.

As I blinked, flakes of ash faintly rained, flittering while they fell.

"It's not a welcome hour, ma'am," the rider said. "Too late to be about."

"I am restless, sir," I replied, "sifting the sands of memory; holding discourse with the deceased. And what business brings you, if I may ask? Isn't the battle at your

back?"

The old man grunted. He scratched the wattle beneath

his beard. "Was," he confirmed as he glanced to the glowing

sky. "Wilson's lost his horse but got himself a bridge. Bad

bargain for us." He sighed. "Pushed his troops across the river

and done the same as Sherman." With an arthritic finger, he

pointed to the flickering aura above the world's edge. "They

laid Columbus to her pyre. Come the dawn, what you knew

of her will belong only to one of those niggling memories of

yours." He grimaced, compounding the many folds to his

face. "What's left of the regulars will join up with Johnston, I'd

think. And what's left of the volunteers will do the same.

That's if we can find him." His bloodshot gaze turned upon

me. Trickling tears sparkled on his pitted cheeks. "But you

ought to know, ma'am, honestly, our sacred war against

aggression …." Dry-mouthed, he swallowed. "We've boiled

our belts for breakfast; our ammunition is nearly spent; and they took what ground we ever got. One of ours is worth ten of theirs, that I'll swear, and none of them is half the shot. But Billy Yank won't stop coming." Without humor, he grinned. "You cut down one, and three more sprout. We just ain't got the wind. The boys is homesick—and tuckered to the bone. And the dead, well, you must know if you've been talking to them: the dead, they just want to forget." He sniffled, and then cleared his throat. "You'd best keep out of sight. Bury whatever you can't spare and nail down the rest." He shook his head. "There'll be plenty eager to take advantage. By the coming rise, I'd expect you'll see a host of blue-bellies blanketing your countryside. Arm yourself which way you can. And pray." He tipped his hat yet again. "I wish you better, ma'am. God's mercy."

With a press of his knees, he urged his reluctant mount back into motion. Skirting my pond, he headed opposite to the direction from which he entered.

"Amen," I muttered as I crossed myself in prayer. "And on you, Sargent."

As if it saw through me and to what lay at my heels, the old soldier's steed turned its head in passing and fixed me in its gaze. Ringed in white, its black eyes bulged. The horse shook its reins and whinnied—and then bolted to a trot.

At my heels, the strange cadaver sighed, long and heavy.

* * *

Astride his bucking steed, the Sargent wheeled. With one hand, he yanked upon his reins and struggled for control. With the other, he drew his revolver—and then took aim.

"WHO GOES THERE?!" he demanded.

I stumbled forward, palms raised in supplication. "Calm yourself, sir!" I hesitated, not wanting to advance too far. Only the spread of my skirt shielded the deceased against perception. I couldn't risk an unveiling. I feared what this slaughterer-of-men might do—whether to me or to my guest.

My spine stiffened. As though I scolded a wayward child, I quipped: "The dead can do you no harm!"

That's right, my daughter's specter eagerly whispered in my ear. *Kill him!* As always, Gigi's hunger boiled. As always, she spoke only to me. As always, I'd rather she kept quiet.

Momma, she insisted, giggling, *slit his throat! Make him bleed!*

I clenched my teeth. "Behave," I whispered huskily to the emptiness at my elbow.

"Is that so?" the Sargent hollered while he dug his knees into either flank. Yet too distant for acuity's sake, he could not have been privy to any word uttered below my breath. At a diagonal compromised between opposing wills, man and horse staggered toward me. Shaking its mane and snorting blasts of panic, the unhappy steed contested each tug against its bit.

The Sargent kept his weapon raised. From where I stood, the wavering barrel seemed a chasm wide. "Move aside, ma'am."

"No," I replied. "Leave be. You flinch from the wheezes of a corpse."

With his thumb, the Sargent cocked his weapon. CLICK!

My heart hung in mid-beat.

"Move aside!" the Sargent yelled.

Gut him, Momma. Kill him now!

Damn interloper. What choice did he allow? I gripped my skirt and briskly sidled clear. "You see?" I shouted to the

Sargent, spraying my words wet with venom. "He's dead. He plays no part in this conflict. Lower your weapon. Have you no decency?"

Huffing, the Sargent's horse pranced backwards and shivered.

"Sweet Mother-of-Christ," the old soldier cursed. His eyes flared wide. "What is that thing?"

I looked to the hapless figure upon the ground. In the feeble light, his boyish face dimly shimmered.

Across the moon, a shadow passed.

"A promise unfulfilled," I whispered.

* * *

Flakes of ash tumbled and whirled. A rapid knocking, similar to a woodpecker's tap-tap-tap, exploded from the darkness— and then clipped silent. However, other than the usual murder of crows that hunkered in the branches, silhouetted by the red glow of the distant fires, nothing else living but the Sargent, his mount, and I were even present.

The Sargent stood next to me. Hitched to a fallen tree, his horse waited in the distance. Hoof-to-hoof, the restless steed shifted. Its long tail swished. Tall and twitching, the horse's ears swiveled in our direction.

"You're the one they call the Hag," the old soldier said, his tone thick with accusation. Dried by worry or fatigue, his voice cracked. With one eye, he squinted. Up and down, he surveyed, assessing me anew. "Ain't that right?"

Now that I saw him closely, he had the look of one who was fond of his liquor. His skin appeared pickled; his nose was bulbous and inflamed; and his gestures lacked certainty. Moreover, his words dragged, ever-so-slightly slurred. But if he had in fact imbibed of late, I caught no scent of it.

I stared at him, denying a reply.

Nervously, he licked his lips. "I heard you're a witch."

"You've probably heard a great number of foolish things," I snapped. "But my situation is misconstrued. And my neighbors speak without charity. Or foundation."

"Yeah, it's got to be you." He lifted his cap and scratched the bald summit beneath. "This is the place. I remember marking your pond when we first passed." Squinting, he looked to me again. "I heard about you, you see?"

"Did you?" I replied.

"The Hag; she walks at night; and for her sins, her crops have all gone to seed." He nodded. "That's you." He looked at the figure lying upon the ground. "Mister Scratch is it?"

"What?" I mumbled. Coals of ire smoldered inside my gaze.

"Lucifer. You know." He waved his hand emptily. "The Devil."

"Satan you say?" I coughed on a laugh—and then crossed my arms and scowled. "The Father of Lies? In my yard? Dead as Sunday's roast? That's what you think?"

"I don't know what to think." The old soldier cleared his throat. He rubbed the back of his neck and frowned. Dubious, he glanced to me again. "If not the Devil, a demon?"

"Don't be a fool," I scoffed. "When have you ever seen a demon—other than at the bottom of your whiskey?" I sneered. "The only *demons* are those we harbor in our hearts."

Icily, the Sargent glared. "Are you not a Christian?"

"You doubt?"

"You harbor demons," he replied. "Said so yourself."

"Don't be obtuse!" Contemptuous, I snorted. "It was a metaphor. I meant the only *real* demons are those born of our guilt over the evils we have committed. They exist only in our conscience." I shook my head. "Use your eyes. He is as real as you or me. And without precedent. Where you perceive the diabolical, I see a gift from God." Inside the furnace of my

regard, I cremated the old fool. "He deserves reverence. Not

suspicion."

The Sargent scratched his chin. "You believe in

miracles, eh? Yet, you don't believe in the Devil? Even when

he is here exact? Horns, hooves, half-man, half-beast?" He

gritted his teeth. "And you, you hid him." A threat for

violence uncoiled from his bloodshot gaze. "Tell me, witch: is

he your master? What pact did you make?"

"Sir!" I slapped my hand to my heart. "You stray too

far from reason!"

"When the asylum breaks, all of us are madmen." He

squatted next to the cadaver, and looked it up and down.

"This is madness, if madness ever was."

He wants to die, Gigi hissed in my ear. *Bleed him till he's*

pretty. Her icy breath caressed my cheek. Along my spine, I

tingled.

As if to make certain it was really there, the Sargent touched the corpse's chest. After a moment, he shook his head. Then, he withdrew and tentatively rubbed his thumb across his fingertips. "I seen men all tore to pieces; they bellies inside-out; throats slit and fizzling a bloody spit. I've heard them beg for mercy. I've stabbed, I've slashed, and I've shot. I've burned, and I've strangled. I've done all that. And I've done worse." He sighed, weaving as he stood, clutching his knees for support. "I shouldn't judge, I suspect." Head down, he chuckled, harmonious to the snuffling of a pig. "Don't figure Old Scratch got a need to make a deal with the likes of me." With a crooked grin, he answered my confusion. "Owns my soul already, see?"

At first, I didn't know how to answer. The red sky cast the faintest glow. A crimson blush tainted everything. And still the sky's ashen tears slowly flittered. In silence, the world slumbered.

"Then do what's right," I finally advised. "If you would atone, help me dig a grave. Let us lower this lost spawn of heaven to his rest."

The old soldier sprung upright. In three steps, he rushed so close that the tide of his heat slammed through me. "Lost spawn?" His brows tightly cinched. "Do not mock me, woman. Speak plainly. Fallen angel is what he is."

My chest seized so tight that I could not breathe. I blurted, "No, that's—"

"You want me to help you return a fiend to his pit?" Even in the gloom, the darkening of the Sargent's complexion could not be missed. A flood of rage flushed across his face.

When in his saddle, the big man had ridden large. Boots to ground, he still loomed above my head. I arched my neck and raised my eyes to confront his scalding temper. And I feared to turn away. At the back of my throat, my tongue bloated numb. Fistfuls of cotton seemed to clog my gullet. Long and hard, I gulped.

Gigi snickered. *I warned you*, she said.

And Gigi was right. This man was a killer. He reeked of stale sweat, dried blood, and brittle danger. With the desperation of the defeated and the lucidity of a rabid beast, he stared into my eyes as though he stripped my soul.

Head-to-toe, I wilted. A cold like a wash of melted snow crept over me.

"Our world has gone to hell," the Sargent said with a snarl. "And there has to be a reason." He grabbed me by my shoulders and squeezed so hard that I thought my bones must split. "God would *not* turn his back on us!" he bellowed. "He wouldn't!"

My tongue throbbed to the beating of my heart. My pulse deafened me. "Sir, please—"

"The victories of our foe are the work of the Antichrist!" the Sargent yelled, incensed by his epiphany. "I see that now. The proof lies before us." His wild eyes sparkled. "It was under our noses all this time." He shook me so hard that my teeth clacked together. Pins of agony pierced my jaw. "Witch!" he cried. "It's you, isn't it? You're at the heart of it."

Mouth gaping, I stared. Breathless, I could not speak.

"You are in league with the Devil," the zealot exclaimed. A man forged by brutal war and by a life of menial labor, he was far fitter than his age might otherwise allow. And his ardor bolstered the strength which god had given him.

Easily, he lifted me off my feet.

All around, showers of ash yet fell. The terrain wallowed beneath a coat of grey.

I gripped the old man's wrists and struggled for release. As tight as a lock that had rusted shut, he held onto me. "Don't be a fool," I stammered. "Let go!"

Inside my captor's eyes, stormy clouds of folly swiftly churned. But the Sargent's expression remained a glyph without translation. He grunted what I can only assume was a recognition. Yet, within his gaze, I saw him splinter.

Without a word of warning, he hurled me away.

I screeched through the empty black. At a jolt, I landed on my heels. Every joint from knee to neck mutely screamed. I stumbled backwards and nearly fell. At my calves, waters splashed as I slid off the sloping shore. Below the surface, the muddy bed engulfed me to my ankles. I flailed for balance. Finally, I found my center. Shocked and terrified, I lifted my gaze to my tormentor.

"What else could that thing be?" the soldier asked as he staggered in my direction, as graceful as a drunken bear. Into the rippling pool, he stomped. "Why else is it here?"

Even as I trembled, I whimpered, "Please, sir, I have no explanation—"

"Of course not." He pointed to the cadaver. "Prince of Darkness! King of Hell! The Serpent and the Beast!"

My spiraling thoughts collided. I was old and frail and all alone. What was I to do?

But then, quicker than a blink, I relaxed. I had reached a verdict. And with the ascent of that conviction, my face hardened into steel.

My decision was simple: I hated this dolt. He and his fears, his superstition and his lunacy, stood between me and my guest. After so many years of exhausting war and endless tragedies, I could forgive nearly any crime. But to defame the defenseless, a manifestation of the divine, a pearl of creation, and the only miracle of its kind that I or anyone else was ever like to see, was an act too perverse to be allowed.

How dare this mongrel, this sot, this vagrant, this ne'er-do-well who'd lost his manners and become a brute, be so utterly stupid? How dare he be so vulgar? How dare he lay his hands on me? The soured scent of his unwashed wool and the pungent sweetness of the gore leaking from his chest turned my stomach. My tongue burned with the bitter taste of bile. His voice rankled reason. His sagging face throttled the last drips of my composure.

Kill him!

"BE STILL!" I bellowed.

"I'll speak when and how I please," the Sargent grumbled. He wagged his knobby finger. "No witch is my better."

"Not you," I fired back. "Her!"

Suspiciously, the Sargent peered to either side and then looked again at me. "What are you on about?"

I shook my head. "Pray you don't discover," I counselled, growling like a cornered cat. I clenched my fists at my sides. In unison, ten knuckles popped. I bit my lips and flinched. "It's clear, sir, why you've never achieved a higher rank," I bitterly declared. "You haven't the faculties to be shrewd."

Specks of ash spun in pirouette. Out of the airy whirl, wafers settled in my hair and dappled my arms and neck. In drifts, the ground ever brightened over shades of dusty grey.

The Sargent tensed. For a sliver of an instant, I thought he might draw the enormous Bowie from the sheath at his belt. He lurched forward, and his gnarled hands curled into clubs. But he stopped before he completed his second step.

Abruptly, he laughed. "Is that so?" he asked with a sneer.

"It is," I said. Fury shook me whole. My teeth chattered. "An ass serves best when it follows; not when it leads."

Stab and stab and stab again! Sixty-four in one night! Oh, the sticky-sticky! Wet candy warm between our fingers! A crimson syrup glaze! Raucous, Gigi laughed. As though they chorused approval, the crows all cawed excitedly from their perches. From far away, a low thump of artillery reverberated. *He wants to play! Oh, let him play! Momma, look and see! It's been so long! Dearest, please, take his hand and dance!*

From the lobes of my ears and to the tips of my toes, every nerve expired. Into a cloud of limbo, I dissolved.

* * *

"I ain't got time for the likes of you." The Sargent trudged up the embankment. Out of the shallows, his footsteps splashed. "Gift or curse, even a *dead* Devil could have his use." He spat a wisp of ash from off his lips. "The enemy is on his way and can't be let to have it, even if just for the pleasure of possession." He approached the corpse. "Your strange companion must come with me. The Old Man should see it, so he might reckon our advantage—if there's any to be had."

Rumbles of bombardment rolled from afar. The muddy earth shook beneath my feet.

This surly brigand! Were there no bounds he wouldn't cross? "By what right?!" I demanded. My left eye ticked. At my ear, Gigi giggled. The crows cawed. Stepping high, I sloshed through the pool. My arms swung wide. As from a pummeling by cannon-fire, spray erupted off my stride. "The discovery is mine, not yours! You have no claim!"

"Better me than Lincoln," the Sargent said, still showing me his back. "Are you a patriot or no?"

I sputtered, "Since when does a miracle hold nationality? His soul belongs to God!"

"A demon has no soul."

"He is no *demon!*"

"WITCH!" the old soldier roared as he spun about. "You mock the resurrection. Am I blind? Is that what you think?! You would have us entomb the Antichrist beside this lake of fire and watch him rise again. That's your trick!" He stabbed his finger toward my pond, where the sky's red reflection weakly glimmered.

At the water's edge, I stood dripping. "You're mad," I proclaimed, so hoarse I could hardly speak.

"No." The old soldier shook his head. "No," he repeated. "I won't have it be for nothing. The years. The lives. My sons. All who fought and died." He licked his lips. "I've slaughtered boys who never grew their first whisker." He looked to me, eyes wide with horror. "You see? This monster could be the reason, whether you're a part of it or no. Or maybe it's our relief." He shrugged. "More than I can figure." Once more he shook his head, and his haggard face fell slack.

"But I won't have it be for nothing. And you, you'll not interfere. Test me and you'll find out."

He turned away once more and grabbed the corpse. He heaved it across his shoulders.

Frantic, I stumbled forward. "You aren't the only one feeling scourged for their survival. You're not the only one in need of purpose after all they had was taken." Heedless, he started walking. I trailed him, dripping as I stepped. "Years ago, this plantation was full of life. Singing! And laughter like you never heard." Dewy-eyed, I smiled. "I even miss the arguments. Even the passing sorrows. Everywhere you went, you'd find someone. People talking. Humanity." Although I raised my skirt to keep from tripping, I still stumbled in the soldier's wake. "These grounds were nothing as they are now: a graveyard for misery, desolate and vacant."

Grunting beneath his burden, the Sargent still ignored me. He steered toward his steed.

Liquid black, the horse's crazy eyes stared at me.

I couldn't keep up with the Sargent's pace. Heavily soaked, my petticoat once more snagged my toes. But I could not allow this dullard to depart—not while in custody of my treasure. In a panic of desperation, I yelled to him, "She killed them, don't you know?" As if possessed by a will of their own, my words erupted, flung on a geyser of guilt. "In one night, my Gigi killed them all." Over waves of sorrow, my sight quickly blurred. "She drugged them into sleep. And cut their throats. Everyone but me. Sixty-four souls. Gone in a single night." The salt of my lament burned upon my lips. "What is a mother to do? She would have swung from the gallows. She would have been reviled and disclaimed. Not even a Christian burial. It was better our name be judged suspect rather than it be damned with certainty." As dry as a shake of gravel, I laughed. "I buried the bodies. Man, woman, and child. In my fields. Day-after-day, I dug. Even after the sun set and the moon cowered beneath the brink, I dug. My palms scarred with blisters. I nearly broke my back, but I did them right. I paid the respect they were due." My throat constricted. "Nonetheless, I remain a sinner. And I have been given one last body to bury."

Momma, Gigi whispered between her giggles, *we danced. We played. I set them free. Why are you so sad? Silly, silly girl.*

The horse whinnied. Ash flurried. Still far away, the batteries of cannons boomed.

"She had to be punished!" I shouted. In a burst of pandemonium, the crows jeered, their laughter a discordant jubilation ringing caw, caw, caw. A noise like thunder rumbled: the heavens splitting. "I had no choice. I held her under. Here. In my pond. Her neck, soft and warm. Manacled between my hands." Bounced from my trembling tongue, my testimony warbled. "Her terror. In her eyes. On her twisted, little face." My shoulders sagged while I withered. "How she kicked. And her screams bubbled around my wrists." Weakly, I held my forearms in front of me, tendering their inspection. "Hours passed before her convulsions ceased. Days, weeks, and seasons. But still I didn't let her go. I held on, making certain." My sight melded with the falling ash. "It was my duty to make certain." All before me shimmered. Black-to-white. White-to-black. At every point of my view. "And ever since, in every day and every night, I beg God for absolution." At that instant, I yearned to be transformed into one of these carefree flakes, one among the many. I'd have welcomed losing myself in such mindless revelry. I envied the anonymity of their communion. "I am sentenced to solitary confinement. It is my penance. And I serve as caretaker to a necropolis of unmarked graves—to atone for what my daughter did." As much to the universe as to the old soldier, I shrieked:

"WHAT MORE WOULD YOU ASK OF ME?"

The Sargent had stopped walking, as had I. Motionless, he still listened, a wall of black standing within a storm of cinder.

Shuddering, I rubbed my hands along my arms, chafing them for the warmth robbed from my circulation. Rasping, I continued, "I ended her spree. No one with any mercy in them could say that I haven't paid the price." Firmly, I shook my head to refute the notion. "Now, in my twilight, when I thought I would end my days without pardon, this blessing came to me. Is he my sign? Am I at last forgiven?" I sniveled. "Do you understand? You steal my redemption from me!"

Quaking as in a seizure, I stretched my arms to the old soldier and begged his pity. "He is meant for me—and for no one else."

At first, I saw only the swirling downpour and the Sargent's silhouette immersed therein. Suddenly, his countenance plummeted from my sky. I didn't even see him turn around before he closed to within an inch of my startled gaze.

He dropped the corpse at my feet. Briefly, I knew a hint of hope. But I had mistaken defiance for a gesture of compassion.

"What daughter?" the Sargent yelled. "You think *witch* is all they called you? Eh, *spinster*? Your suitors fled when you were still a darling, ain't that so?" Merciless, he chuckled. "When you were a girl still budding on the vine." He poked his finger into the dimple below my throat. "Maybe there was talk about a barber who scraped away indiscretions. Now and again, he bled some foolish, young lady barren. Maybe you was—"

NO!!! Gigi screamed.

"SHUT YOUR FILTHY MOUTH!" I bellowed.

I slapped him hard.

And then, the towers of heaven crumbled. Their broken stones passed through me. Within the shadows of the trees, an infant wailed—although I alone could hear it.

SMACK! Reality exploded between my ears. My sky collapsed, and my head whipped to one side. I had not seen the blow coming, just an elbow passing.

The Sargent's fist plowed across my face. I heard a savage crunch. A petal of crystal smashed by an iron mace, my cheekbone shattered. Sparks burrowed through my eye. Agony split my teeth.

Enraged, Gigi howled. *KILL HIM! KILL HIM NOW!*

Instinctively, I raked my fingers across my assailant's inky gaze. I gouged furrows down his cheek.

The Sargent leaned away and cursed—and grappled

for my wrists. The heavens fractured yet again when the old

soldier butted his forehead against my brow.

A thousand shards of light exploded.

And then, my feet no longer touched ground. Exactly

how, I do not know, but the Sargent threw me. Backwards,

I descended. Every ounce of his prodigious bulk fell on top of

me.

Screaming an incoherent cry, I flailed with my fists.

The Sargent wedged his knee between my legs.

Ratcheted to a higher pitch of terror, I screamed yet again.

He seized me by my throat. First with one hand, and

then with both, he choked me into silence.

"No more lies, Hag!" the old man bellowed. "Not from

you; not from me." Empowered by his rage, he squeezed.

With all his sorrow and with all his loss, he squeezed. "Not

from anyone!"

In a frenzy of terror, I clawed at the Sargent's awful hold. Thrashing, I strained to pull free. But his grip would not be broken. He released one hand from my neck and grabbed my hair. By the roots, he twisted. Every tress untied.

And my world began to shrink.

*　*　*

Overhead, a murmur filled the air, shushing as though a haze of jostling moths gently grazed their wings. Whispers of ash pattered where they landed. I lay upon my back, pinned into the gathering dust. The thin, rectangular windows of the corpse's disconcerting gaze peered through the curtain of falling cinders. He lay within my reach if he would but extend an arm. In the emptiness of his strange regard, unblinking and glazed, I sensed a disappointment that soured over intervals equal to my heart's waning beat. And I also saw therein a wordless reproach.

My miracle knew I had failed him.

In truth, shame would be my slayer, and not the madman on my chest. It was shame that stole my breath. But my disgrace was not yet complete.

"Guard your virtue, girl," my mother used to say. And then she would add, "Without it, you are nothing."

I had been nothing for so long I had forgotten her words till now. And yet, the irony struck me: for what little I was and for all that had been taken from me, I still could be reduced to less.

The Sargent tugged. My bodice ripped. Buttons flew. I shook in concert to the old soldier's grind. My fingers were insensate as they fumbled at my neck and pulled on the Sargent's iron wrist.

But still, he strangled me. Even as he reached below my waist and tore my gown and pushed my petticoats aside, he strangled me.

Long ago, they called me fetching. After the decades had leeched me dry, could there be anything left to be claimed as beauty? What flame could a woman of my years ignite? Was I not just as ugly as I was ancient? Time takes all. Age consumes even our dignity. Toward the end, all we have are our memories—and then those too are taken from us. Events escape recollection. Faces once familiar fade until forgotten. Voices from the past dwindle until they are no more than a feeling in our gut. Sometimes, you even doubt yourself. You ask: who am I? The mirror presents an image you no longer recognize. Is that spotted thing really me? How did my life elapse so fast? Why did so many goals go unaccomplished? Why were so many wishes denied? And when all is tallied, what legacy have I left?

But now part of me wondered, more than anything, why did the Sargent bother to treat me so? This farce would be laughable if it was not so degrading—and not killing me.

But I knew my abuse was not born of lust nor was it anything remotely like love's passion. Had I thought about it, I might have felt sympathy. The Sargent's real desire was to extinguish his agonies: his miles and miles of unbearable loss for which no reparation could ever suffice. To restore his pride, he needed to hurt and to humiliate, just as he felt hurt and humiliated. His abuse was a statement, an act of domination. By his will, I was to submit. Yield or die. Through me, he would instill order over the anarchy of his universe.

To make himself right for an act he knew to be wrong, he must also make me less than human. He must make me less than nothing. Who better than a witch?

None of this was said. Nevertheless, I knew it with every blow, with every ache, and with every awkward plunge of his flaccid member.

His impotence enraged him further.

There was naught I could do to end my desecration.

Even if I could have spoken, no reasoning mattered. No reason. No … no … NO! DAMN YOU! STOP! STOP IT, YOU BASTARD!!!

Maybe my molestation was even a miserable old man's bid for life, a parody of procreation as a rebellion against mortality.

However, amidst the turmoil of my mauling, such ideas played at the back of my mind and not at the front. Most apparent at the time was the Sargent's hatred. It radiated from his violence. It heightened his strength and added mountains to the pressure with which he crushed me. His personal hatred for me was as palpable as his round belly flattening my stomach. I sensed his hatred for his life; his hatred for the war; his hatred for everything; and, most of all, his hatred for himself.

But there were no verifiable answers for this vile act or to any of the questions of Life. There really was nothing but the same questions I'd always known, echoing in my head.

Over-and-over. As if they would play the same tune for all

eternity, and I would be imprisoned in their refrain.

In the face of death, I remained as restless and wanting

as when I was but a girl running through the fields. Clueless.

Full of glee. Tossing dandelions in the wind. I knew infinitely

more now than I did then, but in many ways I was none the

wiser. And still there was a part of me that remained that

innocent child of my youth. She was always there. Behind my

eyes.

And deep inside of me, that untarnished purity, still

naïve in the ways of the world, screamed in abject terror.

What justice was this? What balance would it bring?

Indifferent to my fate, the ash still fell. Still the cannons

boomed. Nearby, the frightened steed whickered.

When all was done, would anyone set me to rest? Or

would the crows feast on my decay? Would anyone read a

prayer to usher me to grace? Would they lay a wreath? Light a candle? Grieve? Or even care? Would worms crawl through my open eyes? Inside my ears? Would I feel them slinking through my thoughts? Would they whisper the wisdom of the grave? Would I at last hold the answers that had evaded me?

However, not even if the Lord himself explained every mystery would my murder be tenable. Death might mean release, for then I might set down my terrible burden. And yet, even if I believed in a chance for enlightenment, I would still be deeply unsatisfied.

I had so many things to do before I died. A body to bury. Sins to atone. My soul to save.

My soul … my soul … to save.

Down a contracting tunnel, I fell. The last grain of my focus dissolved into the surrounding blur. Listless, my limbs drooped. Snared by the ever-shrinking noose, no sound issued from my lips. And my body rocked to the pounding at my groin. No longer hot in my ear, the Sargent's panting receded from my perception.

I was inferior to sand. Old beyond any use. As infertile as a field sown with salt. Dry as the tears of a marble Madonna.

Time to be swept from the stoop. Time to join the shadows.

The many faces of the dead gathered. One-by-one, they leaned over, those I had known who passed before. The circle of specters grew and grew. Man, woman, and child. Young and old. Freeman and slave alike. My friends. My family. All who had died at Gigi's blade.

And in their gaze: pity, recrimination, and a thirst for vengeance never to be quenched.

In tidal waves, I shuddered.

But … my guest … my guest … my …

NO!!! Gigi screamed.

* * *

Across the dark, threads of silver flashed. A razor's song whisked to-and-fro. Off each slicing arc, blood misted. Gore sprayed.

Gasping, I sprang upright. By the lungful, I gulped for air.

Mouth agape, the old soldier gurgled. His eyes bloated in disbelief. Away from me, he reeled, and his hands flew to his throat. But he could not staunch the flow. His history gushed between his fingers. His future poured down his chest.

Across his neck, a weeping line. From the divide, spurts of crimson fired. Frothily, the gash fizzed, pulsing in time to the old soldier's breath.

"Gigi!" I shouted as I coughed. I staggered to my feet. "You mustn't!"

But now the Sargent's Bowie cut across his fingers. Amputated digits sailed.

Off the Sargent's belt, his sheath hung empty.

And Gigi giggled. Feral and free. Joyous in her play.

Oh, Momma, dearest Momma, come dance with me!

Again, the kiss of steel slipped beneath the Sargent's chin, smooth and undeterred. As light as the faintest breeze and as steady as a righteous purpose, each cut glided clean.

The Sargent's steed whipped its head. Rearing and tossing, it snapped the branch to which it was tied. The horse scarpered at a gallop. Still tethered, the broken branch dragged behind.

Motionless, the dead stared, their faces bare of passion. The mayhem of crows cawed. An infant cried. The cannons boomed.

Voracious, the blade cut. Back-and-forth, back-and-forth, and back-and-forth again.

Wheeling nowhere, the heavens spun. Gigi laughed.

And then I heard something that I could not

understand. It took me a moment before I figured out what it

was:

Someone else laughed with Gigi. They laughed long

and hard.

And that someone was me.

* * *

The world awoke to a shock of silence. Ash no longer fell.

Patched by sinuous dunes of snowy cinder, the landscape

began to brighten. A smoky bruise veiled the dawn. Behind

the morning's haze, God's angry eye, red and glaring, slowly

climbed. Infinite clouds filled the sky. Here and there,

cerulean rifts gradually pierced the grey. Out every gap,

a shaft of radiance erupted. Without exception, one-by-one,

each beam extinguished, as if what they lit below was too

repugnant to be witnessed.

Synchronous to the break of day, warmth swelled upon my back.

I don't know when the dead had withdrawn, but I was grateful not to weather their censure. Still, although they were unseen, I felt as if they listened.

With gritty scrapes, my shovel bit the earth. Heels-to-hip, the pit in which I stood consumed me. Above, a little knoll piled higher, growing with my shovel's every swing.

Adjacent to that mound, my petticoats lay where I had discarded them. A muddy crust stained the frills in shades of bile-yellow. The rags looked like a carcass with a ruptured chest. Arches of each hoop's broken ribbing jutted between the folds. Ivory-white, the curves of whalebone starkly contrasted against the upturned earth.

Despite the split in the crotch, I still wore my drawers under the remnants of my skirt. Except for the last button before my waist, my bodice flapped free. When I leaned over, my chemise sagged, and my shriveled teats peeked above the neckline.

But I didn't concern myself with modesty. I concentrated on my labors. And Gigi hummed a lullaby that I favored when I was still a girl.

I heard a stiff snap. From the edge of my spade, a slight tremor ran up the handle and through my fingers.

Abruptly, Gigi's ditty ended.

"There you are, my darling," I said. Triumphant, I smiled.

Slanting rays of sunlight now grazed my shoulder. Inch-by-inch, an aura of red crept down the hollow. Slowly, the infection of the tainted dawn descended. Hugging one wall, the roots of an oak that had been toppled long ago branched like the gristle in a slab of jerky. Their shadows warped and crawled. Plastered by clumps of soil and tarnished by decades of seeping rains, moldering layers of bone emerged from the other sides. Here, an arm; there, a foot; phalanges and a pelvis.

Delicate and white, the side of a skull, smaller than my fist, bulged out the muck at my feet. Even after all these years, a few shreds of a burlap shroud still remained.

"Sweet pea," I said, "Momma has brought you a friend."

You mean the goat-man, don't you? Gigi sulked. *Why should I share my bed with the likes of him? He won't dance.*

"Hush," I admonished. "God sent someone nearly as special as you to keep you company."

I liked the soldier better, Gigi curtly replied.

I smirked. "I know, my dear. But this boy needs us. And we need him. Together, we three shall be whole."

The Sargent's blood had drenched me. Ash, dirt, and debris congealed in the sticky mess. My ruffled hair billowed in one direction and knotted in the other. I looked like a threadbare doll ripped at the seams, soaked in the troughs of

an abattoir, and dredged in grime.

And I still smelled the Sargent's rancid veneer, the

musk of his perspiration, his gore, his bladder, and his bowels.

I had steeped in his bouquet, and his odor permeated my

pores. Not only did I inhale his essence, but I exhaled it as

well. Rather than being nauseated by the possession, I felt

drunk. Giddily, I chuckled. Along the border between fatigue

and exhilaration, I wandered, first stepping in one country

and then the other. My poor old muscles were sore. But

I couldn't rest. No, no. Not now. No time to waste.

Gathering my energies, I struggled out of the hole,

grabbed my hard-won prize by his hooves and dragged him

to the edge of my daughter's pit.

Nearby, the Sargent draped over a wheelbarrow. But

he had to wait his turn. Beyond his sleeves, his arms had

blanched to a pasty white. Yet, from wrists to nails, he

blackened. Over the barrow's sides, his four limbs dangled.

His clot-caked fingers hung inches above the ground. Their

stumps still slowly dripped. Likewise, his feet suspended.

Although his eyes stared emptily, he seemed at peace—even

when a large crow landed in the bloody mire upon his chest.

Ear-to-ear and throat-to-spine, the Sargent's neck widely

parted. The bird pecked at a flap of fat. It jiggled. If the old

soldier objected, he kept his disapproval to himself.

Bored, Gigi resumed her humming.

I kneeled. First I wiped the sweat off my forehead with

the back of my arm, and then I braced myself for the coming

effort. With all my feeble strength, I shoved my redemption

across the precipice.

Into silence, he fell. Down and down, he fell. Miles he

fell. Deep into the chasm. Always looking up at me.

Enveloped by the red. Swallowed by the black. To the bottom

of the abyss.

His impact was hushed. On a soundless sigh, the pit expelled a puff of dust.

The clouds began to dissipate. At first as hesitant as a purchased bride, the firmament disrobed. Blue, its naked skin gleamed. My plantation brightened. The sun shucked its crimson sheen in favor of a blazing yellow.

The crow standing on the Sargent's chest screeched once and spread its wings. Sunlight brushed its feathers an iridescent green. As if afire, the big bird launched. Through the air, it complained. The rest of the flock cawed furiously and followed in retreat.

Off my shoulders, a yoke of worries seemed to lift. From far away, I heard a dog bark. I even thought I heard the velvet chirping of a thrush.

Snuffed like a candle, Gigi had snapped silent.

And the crows winged away, shrinking until they vanished; their flock, a crowd of smoke dispersed by a welling breeze.

I looked at the sky like I'd never seen it before, or rather like I'd seen it so long ago that it struck me as something new. And yet, it tugged at my memory. When had the heavens last seemed so unencumbered? Had the world ever been so bright? Maybe once. When I was young. While I was embraced in a moment of sorrow beneath the last sun of summer.

"Everything will be all right," Gabriel had promised me. He stroked my hair while I wept. His chest was warm beneath my cheek. His muscles, my pillow. I heard his heart beating, strident as a drum. I don't think even in our youthful naiveté that either of us believed what he said, but it was all he had to offer. In his arms, I always felt safe, no matter our danger. The love we shared was our shelter.

How I longed for his claim to be true. We had barely begun our fate together. If the world had been right, our hope should have been endless. But everything was all wrong—and nothing would ever be right again.

What fools we were. We knew too well our affections could never be declared in public. We'd never be let to live as husband and wife. Our union was founded on the most ardent devotion but would be denounced as an abomination.

I wish we had found the strength to run away. But we were each trapped in worlds of our own. He was cursed for his race. And I was cursed by class and the proprieties of prejudice. We both were shackled to familial obligations. But where our worlds overlapped, we convened; ever discrete outside and hushed behind closed doors.

I never confessed who he was. Not when I became ill and my mother interrogated me. Not when my belly began to swell. Not when my father beat me. Not when I was locked in my room and sequestered from our neighbors. Not when my sisters bound and gagged me and locked me in our barn. There, while the horses huffed and snorted and shat in their stalls, I was forced to spread myself before a stranger—and suffer a barbaric surgery. I still did not disclose my lover's name when the butcher showed my parents the motionless remains of the infant whom he had carved from my womb. My baby's dusky pallor was much darker than my own but also much lighter than her father's. In the blessing of her, I saw us both: Gabriel and me, joined as one in our daughter— our daughter who was never born.

I bled. I bled and bled. The knife was gone, but still I bled. My pulse fluttered. And into the twilight betwixt life and death, I fainted.

Three days later, I came out of my coma. During that time, someone had tattled. Perhaps, it was a slave seeking favor who knew when and where my ebony Adonis went in the odd hours of day or night. It could have been a house servant who had espied me sneaking out my window or noticed that I dawdled too long in the cellar. Or maybe one of the overseers had observed us in the woods, an unlikely couple who could never be alone together, the buck and the belle.

I never discovered exactly which villain it was. That secret they were able to keep. That person, they protected.

Oh, the Hell that followed. Everyone hated me. My family made me prisoner. Although sworn to silence for honor's sake, the freemen regarded me a whore. They refused to look on me. They spat on the ground when my back was turned. And the slaves despised me for the punishments they endured. Any of them who dared to whisper of the affair never spoke again. Not with their tongue missing. Tempers grew short. Whippings became more common. No one talked to me. Not then. Not even once, through and including the night they all died together.

Only after much begging was I allowed to bury my baby. Too frail to walk after I first awoke, I had to be taken in a cart. And then my sisters propped me upright. Gabriel's mother handed me an old sack that had been used for seed. Therein, I bundled my little poppet and laid her to her earthen cradle. At night. When the stars hung high. When no one would see. In a place that would never be marked. In a place meant to be forgotten.

I recited from the Bible. My hands shook so hard, I dropped it twice. And then I finished with a prayer. But I was the only one to say "Amen." Two tight-lipped slaves filled the pit. No tears but mine were cast. And then I was lugged back to bed.

The ceremony did not sooth me. Gigi was furious. And no one would say where my lover had gone. My forbidden lover. My sweet boy. They told me he had been discovered.

But they pretended that Gabriel had been sold and sent away.

Yet, by their expressions, I knew better. When at last I'd

recovered so far that I could walk without assistance,

I searched the grounds. Desperately, I searched. Yet I never

found where his remains were hidden. I have always

suspected that my father and his men wrapped him in a

blanket weighted with a pile of stones and sank him in our

pond. They had disposed of a litter's runts more than once in

such fashion—the dogs they'd deemed unfit. It couldn't be a

coincidence that our family stopped going there. Or why the

place so drew me. They probably hung him first, deep in the

woods, where there would be no witness. Strangled, he could

not have called my name.

Unable to do aught else, I consigned myself to grief. For

the lover I had lost. For the daughter taken. For the children

I could never have. For the marriage I'd been denied. For the life I should have lived. For my life that was over. And for the guileless girl who'd let her heart sway reason. She would always be my better self. And she was dead, as cold as a corpse bound in ice, deep inside of me.

But she was not quiet.

Through my bitterness, Gigi learned to hate. My family. The freeman. And the slaves. She grew hungry for their blood; so hungry that after years of brooding her night finally came, and I could no longer contain her.

* * *

"Already?" I whispered. My shovel served as the post on which I leaned. With a hand for shade, I squinted against the morning's blare.

Dust announced the coming invasion; followed minutes later by the glints of bayonets and then by the creaks of a score of wagons, the clopping of cavalcades, and the scuffled steps of legions. While I waged a remote witness, the armies of our enemy advanced. Along with the colors of each

unit, the *Stars and Stripes* boldly waved. Tight as rats

swarming through a drain, columns stuck to the roads. But

the scouts and the stragglers did not.

I went back to work, hoping that the jackals would pass

my plantation from afar. I had so much to do. No time for

niceties; and less time for trouble.

However, not long thereafter, the midpoint of my

backbone prickled. A wave of frost chilled me from within,

and a feather of warning caressed my neck. I knew that I was

watched.

Slowly, I turned.

A hundred yards or so away, three Yanks had

dismounted. They walked their lathered steeds across the

empty field and in my direction. I suspect they intended to

water their horses at my pond and cool them in my shade. I

had no doubt that every chart employed by either side noted

every spring and every well for many miles around. As they stumbled, the men and their horses kicked up the dusty earth. Lines meticulously ploughed and then eroded by the seasons now utterly collapsed. As victors, I suppose my callers must have felt entitled to make whatever use of my property that they wished; and to do so without consideration. Oh, the grounds had all gone fallow in another age, I know, but to a planter the land must always be treated like a lady. You don't trample the tillage. Moreover, you don't step into someone's home without first coming through their gate and knocking at their door. You don't enter without invitation. Careless of decorum, the trio had slipped off the public trails and traipsed directly through my land. Such a flagrant faux pas befits only brigands. As my mother used to say, "Rudeness never endears." Already, I disliked our conquerors—almost as much as I distrusted them.

They ported their rifles across both hands, ready to shoot anything that didn't please them. Their heads swiveled anxiously, probably for fear of snipers. Much to my regret, no such intervention relieved me of the nuisance that approached.

The second interment to which I was committed this day wasn't even half-dug. In that shallow trench, I was only concealed from my knees on down. If I was younger, and thus more limber, I might have ducked to my belly. Nowhere else was near enough for me to hide. The closest trees were a long sprint away, and my house was even further. But it was obvious that the invaders had already spotted me anyway. And if I ran now, I would never have made it to shelter before I was caught—or before I was shot in the back.

When the three scruffy, young Yanks got within range of a detailed look, I saw their mouths drop. One crossed himself. Another coughed excessively. And the third swore beneath his breath.

Gummed by gore and filth, a caul of tousled hair draped my face. Sweat scraped muddy runnels through the grime upon my skin. Wearied long past my limit, I slouched. What clothing I had left either stuck to me or hung in tatters. I was bared beyond any standard of decency. Since the rise of dawn, I had been defiled even more terrible. In the blood of carnal sacrifice, I seemed as if anointed to a savage faith. I stood as a pagan priestess. The whore of Babylon. Lilith. Bathsheba. Hecate. The bride of Satan.

The Hag.

Irony slapped me hysterical. I laughed so hard I cried. Just like the witch flying on her broom, I cackled. And then, conscious of that comparison, I looked at the handle of my shovel; and guffawed.

I had become the very thing that years of malicious rumor had named me.

A stone's throw away, the squad of Yanks faltered to a halt. Their horses balked and would come no closer.

"She off her chump?" asked the cougher.

"Tight as a boiled owl," said the soldier who had crossed himself.

The gaze of the rifleman who had spoken in expletives slid off of me and landed on the wet mass in the wheelbarrow. His eyes lit when he focused on the vertebrae at the back of the yawning gash beneath the chin. "Sweet Jesus," the young officer exclaimed.

The other riflemen snapped their heads to where their leader looked. They dropped their reins and jammed their rifles against their shoulders and squinted down their barrels. Fingers tensed on triggers.

And then they understood the contents of the barrow.

Unraveled by dismay, their faces sagged. In their wilting arms, their weapons lowered.

"What in the name of …?" the pious Yank inquired of no one. Into the emptiness of horror, he faded.

"Christ," said the foul-mouthed soldier. He was a corporal, if I was to judge by his insignia. The others were marked as common infantry. "What happened here? Ma'am? You hear me? What's your name? Eh? Come now." The Corporal planted the butt of his gun against the ground and propped the weapon upright by its muzzle. "You needn't be afraid. We wouldn't hurt no woman." He smiled in a misconceived attempt to be ingratiating, and thus exposed his missing teeth. "So, what's your name?"

How sheep will bleat. Baa-baa-baa. Baa, little sheep, Baa. I'd had more than my fill of interruptions for one night. Whilst I considered this latest injustice, the strings of an orchestra—at first as mild as the nimbus of a rising moon—

ascended into waltz. On angel's wings, the notes gathered. Soaring. Glorious. Higher and higher.

"Marie," I mumbled. "Marie Georgine Vernieux." Hearing myself, I startled. And then I frowned. That name. It clanged in my ears; congealed on my tongue. Something … odd ….

I set my shovel aside and tried to push myself out of the pit, but my limbs were so tired that every muscle shook as from a seizure, and my feet insisted on slipping. The walls around me crumbled.

Da-da-da-da-da! Da-da, da-da. Da-da-da-da-da! Da-da, da-da. Da-da-da-da-da! Da-da, da-da. DA-DA-DA-DA-DA! DA-DA, DA-DA. DA-DA-DA-DA-DA! DA-DA, DA-DA ….

Round and round, the heavens spun. My eyelids shuddered. But I refused to surrender to my exhaustion. Red-faced and grunting, I scrambled for release, a beetle in a jar.

"Go help her," the Corporal commanded.

The cougher grimaced. "Ah, Hell. Why I gotta—?"

"You seriously going to piss yourself over an old lady?" The Corporal sneered. "Go on, get. The both of you."

Grumbling, the two privates laid down their rifles.

As if in warning, their horses whinnied and tossed their manes. They pranced as though the ground might sink, and took several steps backwards before they settled.

Heads down, the privates had scurried forward. They grabbed me from beneath my arms and grimaced when the grit and gristle slid beneath their fingers.

"Here now, Ma'am. Be careful. Easy."

"Lift … just … yeah, now, lift … no, your foot. That's right." Cough, cough, cough.

My reluctant valets retreated once I stood outside the pit. But not far. They could not wipe their hands soon enough. They could not scrub too hard. Jackets substituted for towels and were quickly stained in streaks. Nonetheless, a tar that would not go away clung between their fingers. Their nails

had been dipped in black. Pitch crossed their knuckles. And

their palms were etched in fractured webs of scabby ink.

"Cripes," said one.

"It's mostly blood," the other whispered. Tentatively,

he sniffed his fingertips. "Blood and dirt and …." He curled

his lips inside his mouth, and then closed his eyes and

trembled—seeming to have concluded that certain truths are

best if left unspoken. They're easier to deny that way. Cough,

cough, cough.

"Thank you, boys," I mumbled. I glanced around to

regain my bearing. My head swam up a muddle. A chain of

knots clenched my spine. Stiff as a broken branch, I could

hardly move; or hardly think. Bursts of pain wrenched me.

"Is this man your kin?" the Corporal asked. He pointed

at the Sargent's corpse.

My eyes followed the Corporal's finger. Propelled by his gesture, I lurched to the wheelbarrow. My hips popped, and I winced. Barely in time to avoid a tumble, I grabbed onto the barrow's edge. As I looked down, my gaze locked upon the Sargent. A thread of spittle dangled from my chin. The glistening strand plummeted. Spatter ran down the Sargent's cheek. Satisfied, I chuckled. But then, a well to nowhere, one of his vacant eyes pulled me in. Down that shaft, I tumbled; down and down and down, falling without end. Through that funnel, I swirled. And for a pause between the minutes, I was young again. A gown like no other flattered my every curve and amplified my pert bosom. Around my neck and from my ears, sprays of diamonds sparkled. I merrily spun, capering through a waltz. Graceful. Without a care. Across a marble floor, I glided. And I laughed. Oh, how I laughed. The laughter of the young. Unencumbered. Still glowing bright with innocence. I was a princess at her cotillion; the belle of the ball. I was the center of the universe. Destiny poised tense, eager to grant me my every wish. At the edge of the gathering, Gabriel stood. His smiling eyes fixed on me while I blushed, gay in my revels, devoid of concern. And on my lover's lips—

"Marie?" the Corporal called. "Are you injured?"

Confused, I blinked. In my ears, the waltz continued. At the edge of my sight, on every side, a commotion of dancers still swept. But I was no longer a participant. I was a rock in a river of memories that flowed around me.

And Gabriel was gone.

Marie? Is that the name I had declared? No, no, that wasn't right. Far too mundane. Georgine? Who could carry such a cross? Too unwieldy. No, something else. Once upon a time, I had another name; at an age when the future balanced upon my whim and life was magical; when every dream was a promise of good fortune. It was the name that Gabriel whispered in my ear; the name by which he wooed me, the name he invoked like the holiest of prayer when we lay in each other's arms, sweating and complete.

And the orchestra grew louder.

Abruptly, I hummed—although not in accord to the spiraling measure of the dance. I hummed a different tune: the lullaby that Gigi had sung. To that tempo, I swayed, out of sync to the rhythm of the waltz. My lips parted; lyrics trickled. It had been so long since last I sang I couldn't remember when it was. But now, I serenaded the baby I'd never dandled on my knee, the baby never held to my breast, the baby I'd never hugged or kissed. I sang the love I'd never had a chance to give. Reedy and off-key, I sang farewell. And a tear meandered down my cheek.

"Marie?" the Corporal prodded. "We can't help if you don't tell us what happened." Concern tipped his lilt just a little higher. "Who did this to you?"

My hand slid into the barrow. From the bottom, I heard the clunk of metal as the instrument my fingers found snagged briefly against the splintered grain of the wooden bed.

Still the waltz continued. And still I sang.

To the Yanks at my back, it must have appeared as if I crooned to the cadaver, as if I thought he was my infant and I'd set him down to nap in his crib.

And then the tableau resolved into perspective. As though I stood outside it, I suddenly understood. I had to laugh. Puppets in performance, the five of us reenacted the Nativity; albeit a *diabolical* nativity, as the Sargent would probably have recognized. The three soldiers, strangers from afar, were the wise men. And the tributes they bestowed? Ignorance, strife, and humiliation. They came at day instead of night, in opposition to the circumstances for our savior. The star that led them was the sun. The barrow was the Manger.

And I, the unholy Hag—my womb, a bag of dust—was mother to this sacrilege. We assembled not for the Messiah, not for the progeny of God, but rather to gaze upon a symbol of desecration. Through his blood, we denounced the miracle of life. Through us, the Fallen mocked the divine. And our homage to this dark faith was paid in human sacrifice: the Sargent, whom we offered on the altar.

"Did you know him?" the Corporal asked.

Ah, you poor little sheep. Still bleating, are you? Maybe this young Turk was homesick. Maybe he saw his own sweet granny when he looked at me. Maybe he imagined her laying his granddad to rest, all alone, with no family or friends to give her comfort or to lend a hand. What if gramps had met such a grisly end? What if nana had been beaten and stripped and submersed in innards? Would she not be shocked as witless as this bony wretch who stood before him now?

Whatever the reason for his interest in me, I don't think I could have cared any less.

No time for niceties; and less time for trouble.

The dagger's handle remained hot, still dripping with the life it spent. The grip felt as familiar as a favorite shoe. The weight, just right. The balance, light and easy on the wrist. The steel, sharp and living. Jubilant. Anxious for another game. To draw threads of silver once more through the air.

The waltz went on. And still I sang. With both hands, I cupped the dagger to my belly.

"Old biddy's lost in the henhouse," the cougher muttered.

"Yeah," the pious man agreed. "Let's get out of here." He gulped. "You notice? Nothing's growing. Not a bush or a weed." He licked his lips. "But outside this plantation, it's all green."

Neither the cougher nor the Corporal responded. I suppose they likewise pondered, in search of cause or meaning.

And although the soldiers and the world had all gone dumb, lullaby still weaved with waltz.

The earth trembled.

Beginning slow and soft, tribal drums now joined the din blowing through my head. Steadily, they beat toward a savage boil. The blood of Africa bubbled in the heat of a mounting conflagration. Fires leapt before my eyes. But the vision was my own. I know that. I know that.

The orchestra yet played oblivious. Mesmerized, I continued to sing, neither raising my voice nor altering the tempo.

Side-to-side, I swayed.

Although the crows had departed, their caws erupted from all around. Off the burning void inscribed by the barrow,

I raised my eyes and found myself surrounded not by dancers but by a host of specters; the plantation's dead, only now rediscovered. Their throng encircled the living. They were as translucent as reflections on a dusty window and as green as the mold in a fetid tomb. Their grim expressions never changed. Their cold eyes smoldered. And none among their congregation uttered even a single word.

"Marie?" the Corporal asked. He set down his rifle, dropped his horse's rein, and stepped toward me. "You can trust us."

Out of the deepest caverns of a frozen Hell, a cold wind blustered. As though they felt it too, the three Yanks shivered. But I heard it whisper: one word; the name that only part of me kept after I'd been splintered.

Whole at last, I remembered who I really was.

I was young and beautiful. My future was a glorious mystery. Life was joy. And my love waited for me.

And I was the daughter I'd never had.

"Gigi," I said. I looked over my shoulder at the three men. Lop-sided, I grinned. "Only my parents ever called me Marie. You must call me Gigi." Flirtatiously, I giggled. And turned around.

"Come dance with me," I said.

Whispering secrets, my blade drew threads of silver through the air.

The wine of the living flowed.

The wise men never stood a chance.

Exulting in the sunlight, I drank from the sky. So hot it was an insult, the day melted into all tomorrows. In Gabriel's arms, leagues beneath the pond, while the screams rang above the waters, I danced away unwanted memories, the faults of another life, and the regrets for all that had been and for all that could not be.

And all around me, the souls of the dead stared in rebuke.

And Gigi was Gigi again.

THE END

COMING SOON *from* **Marc Royston:**

The Wizard Ignites, an adult epic fantasy novel

An Apprentice's Account of Duty, Love and Other Such Calamities

Out of an Inferno, a wizard's life begins.

Accused of being a witch and of murdering the girl he loves, a naïve young farmer faces the terrible cost of his gift for magic. While on trial for his life, Götling unravels a web of intrigues spun by wizards, gods, and royals. If he can overcome his persecutors and gain admittance into the Academy of Arcane Arts, Götling might yet learn to control his fiery power and become the instrument to decide all wars.

The Piper of the Dead invades the Empire. The Shadow Queen and her demon army prepare to escape their long imprisonment. And an insane goddess plots to overthrow her peers.

The time foretold has come. Afire, a reluctant hero rises into legend.

AUTHOR'S BIOGRAPHY

Marc Royston (Artist/Actor/Writer) was born in Atlantis but currently lives in California. He talks to himself a great deal and yells at his computer. As the author of numerous teleplays, screenplays, poetry and fiction, he began his writing career at the age of 6. His earliest drafts were composed in crayon on whatever surface he could find (whether paper, wall, floor, or sidewalk). A fantasist, Marc Royston spends much of his time exploring alternate universes which reflect our own. Through tales of magic and legend, he delves into the intricacies and foibles of human relations amidst the conundrums of modern society.

Quote: "I seek to take my audience on an emotional roller-coaster ride, a journey of laughter and tears and every sentiment in between. I immerse myself and therefore my readers in worlds as familiar as they are wondrous and strange."

Follow Marc Royston at:

Blog: "The Wizard's Workshop"
                www.marcroyston.wordpress.com

Twitter: @MARCROYSTON

Facebook: www.Facebook.com/AuthorMarcRoyston

Amazon: www.amazon.com/author/marcroyston

www.ingramcontent.com/pod-product-compliance
Lightning Source LLC
Chambersburg PA
CBHW071340130626
46556CB00004B/1957